The First

DRAGLINGS™

Coloring Book

For kids of all ages

Artwork by Randal Spangler

Compiled by Leslie Brumagin

randalspangler.com

Welcome to my first Draglings Coloring Book!

I hope you enjoy coloring the Draglings world. You can use your imagination and make each page look as colorful as you want or you can go to my website randalspangler.com for color inspiration. For the best results, put a piece of heavy paper behind the page you're working on to keep markers or paints from bleeding through to the next page.

Check out my children's books and my fine art prints available on my website randalspangler.com

What is a Dragling?

Draglings are small dragons that live mostly indoors in a not-so-far-away place called Ohmlandia. These two Draglings are twins: Dagmar and her brother, Dewey. You can tell them apart by the warts on their cheeks and balls on the ends of their tails: Dagmar has four, and Dewey has five. Draglings are somewhat mischievous. They love to explore attics, read books, and eat choclate chip cookies. Chocolate is a special treat because it doesn't exist in Ohmlandia. Draglings can pass through magical mirrors from their world to ours in search of chocolate. So if you find your cookie jar empty in the morning, you've probably been visited by Draglings.

Celestial Dreams

Draglings dream of the moon and stars
all in colorful jars

A Little Bit of Magic

This Teacup Dragon is studying to learn magic. It's a very colorful occupation

THE LITTLE BOOK OF MAGIC

RARE OLD MAGIC SPELLS

THE COMPLETE BOOK OF SPELLS

A Little Bit of Magic

All Wound Up

The Draglings wind the clocks every day
so they know how much TIME they have
to color and read

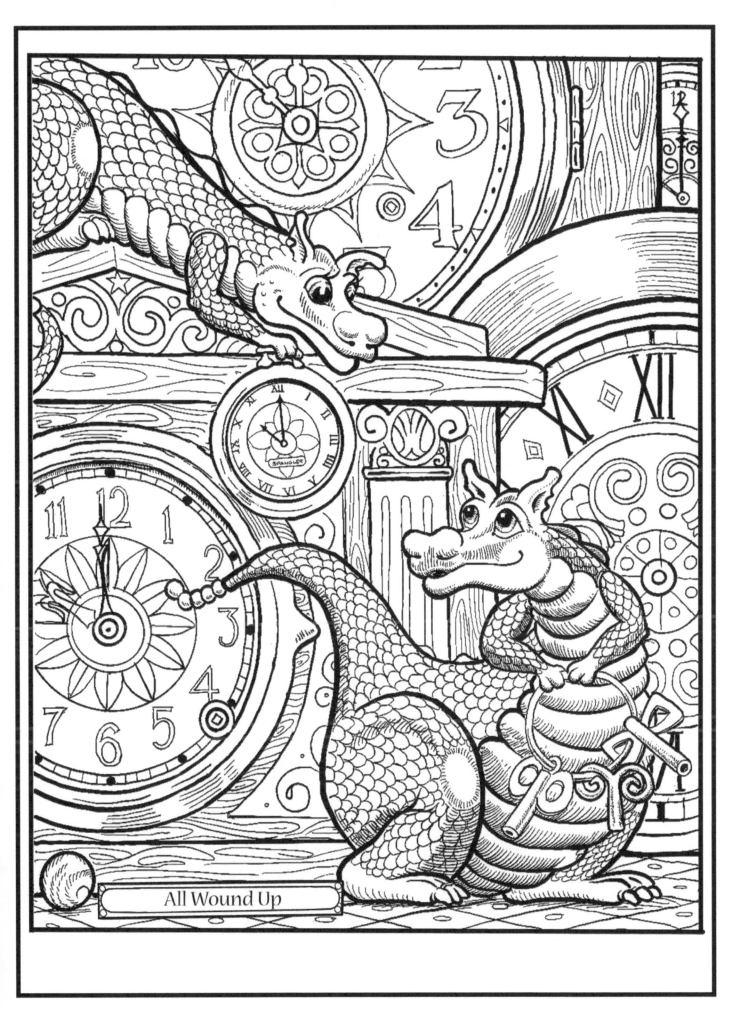

All Wound Up

Cooking by Candlelight

Draglings love chocolate chip cookies
Color your favorite cookies

Cooking by Candlelight

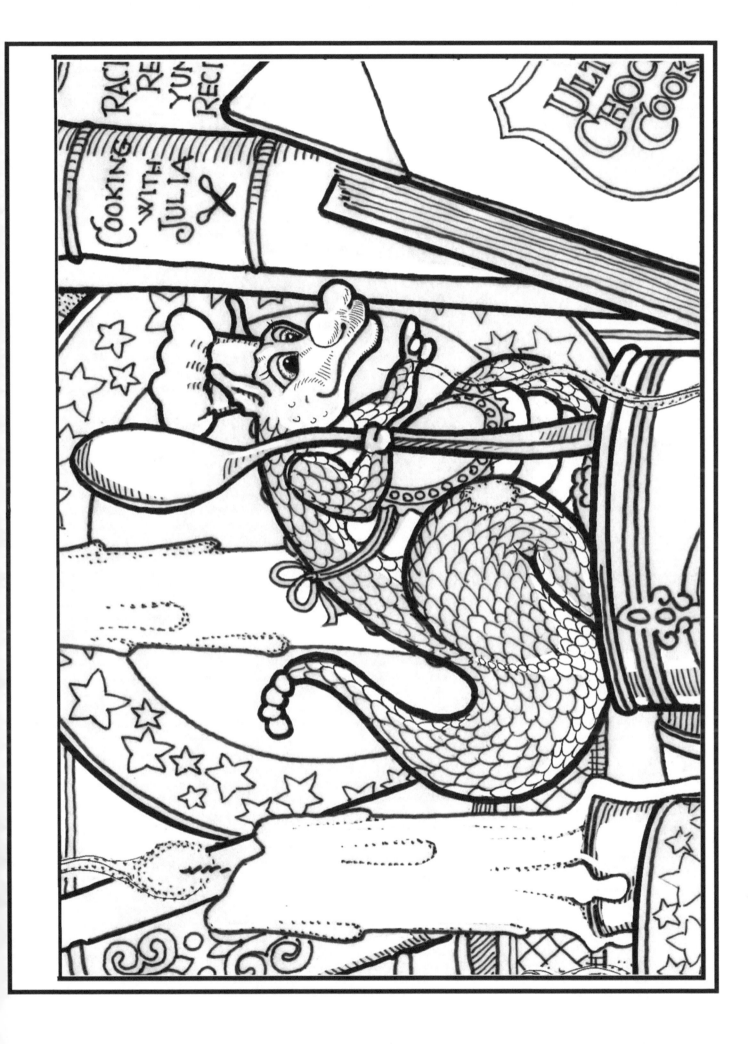

Zoom Zoom

Dewey loves to fly
Give him colorful wings

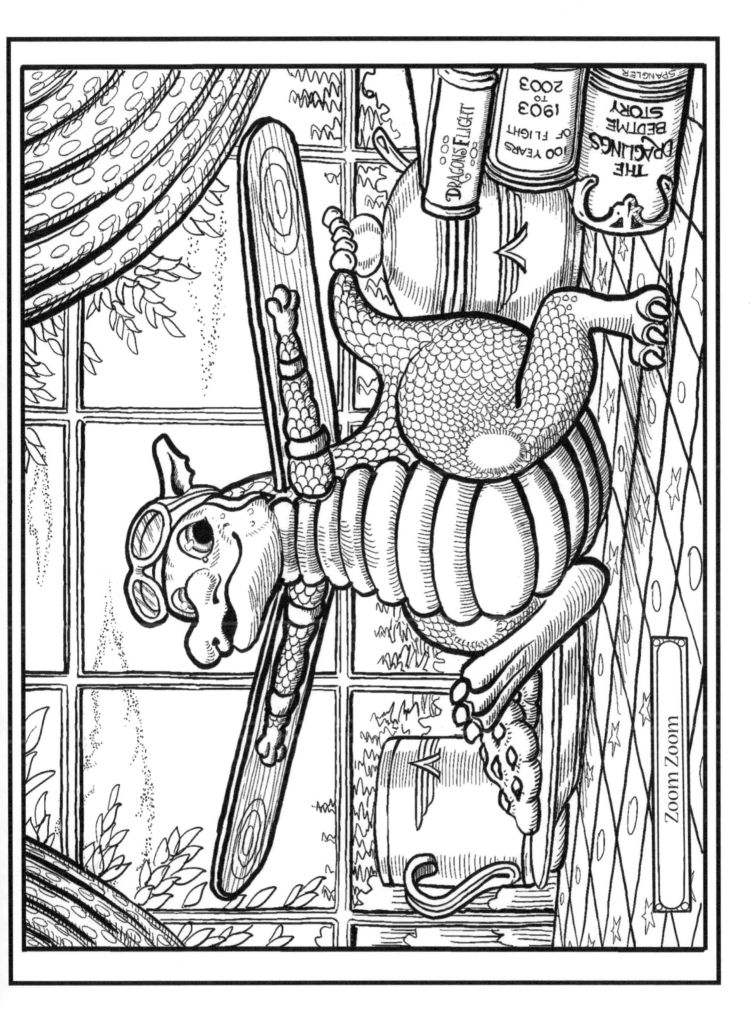

Reading Time

The Draglings love to read
with their many friends in a
colorful forest library

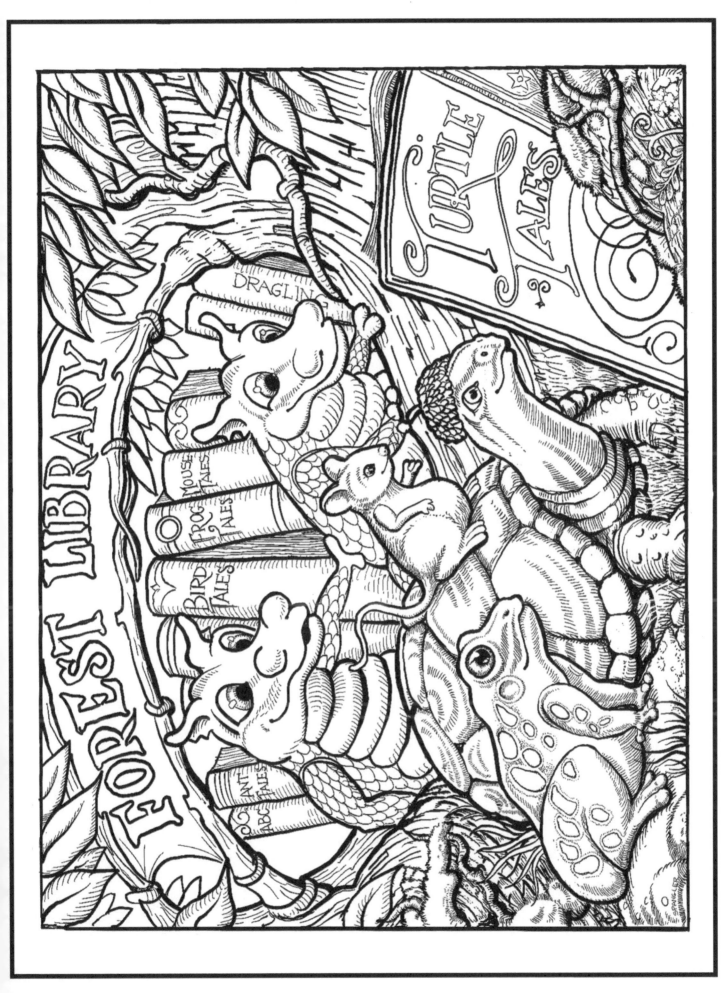

Reading Time

Play Ball!
Baseball is fun for Dewey to play
Color him happy

Play Ball!

Everything's Better with Chocolate Chips On It

Find all the chocolate falling from the sky
and color everything tasty

PEANUT BUTTER

RS

ICE
VANILLA
CREAM

HONEY

Everything's Better with Chocolate Chips on It!

SPANGLER

Good Books Make
Good Friends

*Draglings and books are best friends
Add your favorite titles to the
colorful books*

DRAGON READERS

Good Books Make Good Friends

SPANGLER

Morning Coffee

*A cup of coffee is a good start to
a colorful day*

All Wound Up
The Draglings wind the clocks every day
so they know how much TIME they have
to color and read

All Wound Up

Lazy Day

*Some mornings are perfect for
staying in bed under
a colorful quilt*

THE OLD DRAGON AND THE SEA

Lazy Day

Bedtime Stories

*One last story with a cookie
makes going to sleep so much easier*

Bedtime Stories

Bedtime Stories

So Many Books, So Little Time

Draglings love lots of colorful books
with your favorite titles

Sundae Delight

Ice cream is delicious in a colorful room

Sundae Delight

Train of Dreams
The Draglings have so much fun
on their colorful train

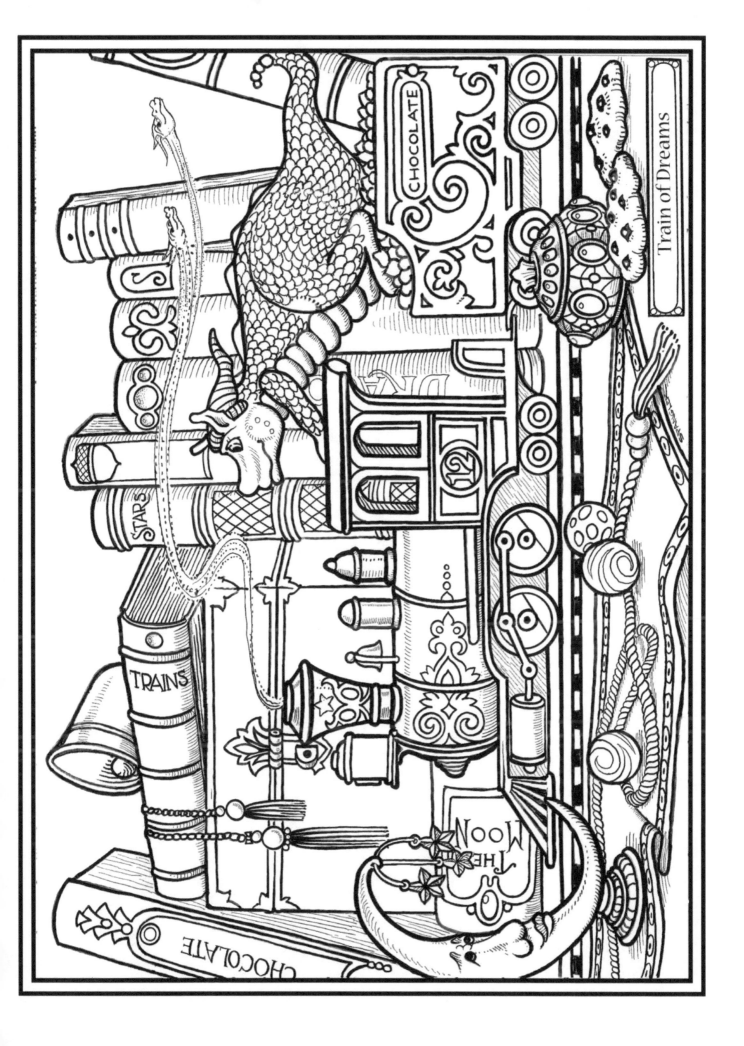

Treasure Quest

Draglings love playing pirates with a
treasure chest full of colorful jewels

Treasure Quest

What Cookies?
Even teacup dragons love cookies
a little too much

Fairytale Dreams

*Dewey is all snuggled up in a bunny
slipper with a firefly night light*

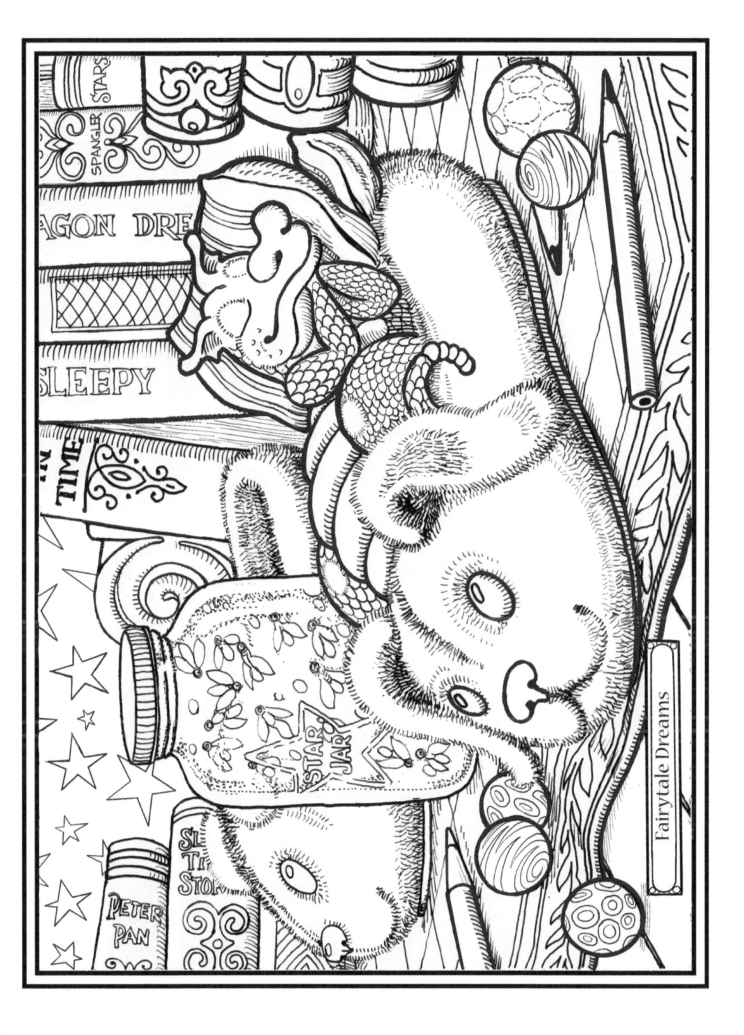

Midnight Munchies

Dagmar thinks a cookie in the middle
of the night is a colorful good idea

Midnight Munchies

Midnight Munchies

Nap Time

With their wings all tucked in
the Teacup Dragons are snuggled
in their colorful teacups

Nap Time

Nap Time

Nap Time

Sleep Tight

*Dagmar and Dewey put their toy dragon
and teddy bear to bed hoping for
colorful dreams*

Sleep Tight

Curl Up with a Good Book

With a colorful drink and a good book
Dagmar settles down with a cookie
to munch on

Curl Up with a Good Book

Curl Up with a
Good Book

Devouring a
Good Book

*Kromwell loves books so much he reads
them and then munches on them as he
sits among his colorful books*

Devouring a Good Book

The Easter Dragon

*Dewey thinks he has a clever plan to
find some chocolate Easter eggs, which
come in lots of colors*

Easter Dragon

Blast Off

Teacup Dragon's wings are too small to really fly, but they keep trying, jumping off stacks of colorful books

The Chocolate Detector

Always in search of chocolate, the Draglings
use technology to help them find it

Chocolate Detector

No More

Dragon Breath

*The Draglings brush and floss every day
so they can keep their teeth healthy
and shiny white*

No More Dragon Breath

It Tastes Better
When We Share

The best way to enjoy a cookie is to share it. You can share this coloring book, too!

It Tastes Better When We Share

Lighting the Way
Into the night Dewey goes with his
acorn light

Lighting the Way

The Dream Staff
Draglings can grant you
colorful dreams

The Dream Staff

Hope you had fun!

Made in United States
Troutdale, OR
11/04/2023

14289299R00051